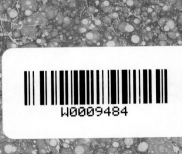

A GUINEA PIG

OLIVER TWIST

A GUINEA PIG

OLIVER TWIST

Or, the Parish Boy's Progress

AN ADAPTATION OF THE ORIGINAL BY

CHARLES DICKENS

LONDON

BLOOMSBURY PUBLISHING, BEDFORD SQUARE.

2016

CHARACTERS & CAST

Oliver Twist
[Oreo]

Mr Brownlow
[Molly]

Mr Bumble
[Sherlock]

Mr Sowerberry
[Mabel]

Mister Noah Claypole
[Cookie]

The Artful Dodger
[Hermione]

Fagin
[Elsie]

Monks
[Doris]

Bill Sikes
[Millie]

Bull's-eye

Nancy
[Billie]

FROM THE WORKHOUSE

3

2

1

TO CHERTSEY AND
THE COUNTRYSIDE

LONDON
AND ITS ENVIRONS

<-+->

1. Fagin's lair,
a low neighbourhood

2. Clerkenwell Green

3. Pentonville

4. London Bridge

[THE WORKHOUSE]

Oliver Twist was born an orphan of the workhouse and fell into his place at once – a parish child – the humble, half-starved drudge – to be cuffed and buffeted through the world, despised by all, and pitied by none.

'We name our foundlin's in alphabetical order,' said Mr Bumble,
the parish beadle. 'This was a T – Twist.'

Oliver's eighth birthday found him a pale, thin boy. Believing that meat made for a rebellious child, the workhouse had a policy of gradual starvation, issuing the children only three meals of thin gruel a-day, with an onion twice a week and half a roll on Sundays.

One evening little Oliver, desperate with hunger and reckless with misery, rose from the table, basin and spoon in hand, and said—

'Please, sir, I want some more.'

The next morning a bill was hung from the workhouse gate, offering a reward of five pounds to anybody who would take Oliver Twist off the hands of the parish.

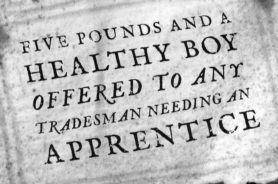

Mr Sowerberry the undertaker decided to take Oliver as his apprentice, but even he was surprised by the boy's appearance. 'Dear me! he's very small,' he said.

'Why, he *is* rather small,' replied Mr Bumble, looking at Oliver as if it were his fault he wasn't bigger.

'Well, come with me,' said Mr Sowerberry, leading the way to his funeral parlour.

'You won't mind sleeping with the coffins, I suppose?'

D ue to his natural expression of melancholy, Oliver was soon accompanying Mr Sowerberry to all manner of funerals.

However, young Mister Noah Claypole, who minded the undertaker's shop, was jealous when he saw the new boy being promoted so quickly. He taunted Oliver in the hope of making him cry, and then, when all else failed, he got rather personal.

'Your mother was a regular right-down bad 'un, work'us,' said Noah,
'and it's a great deal better that she died when she did.'

A minute ago Oliver had looked the quiet, mild, dejected creature that harsh treatment had made him. But his spirit was roused at last; the cruel insult to his mother had set his blood on fire.

Crimson with fury, he started up, overthrew chair and table, seized Noah by the throat, shook him in the violence of his rage till his teeth chattered in his head, and collecting his whole force into one heavy blow, felled Noah to the ground.

'Help! help!' blubbered Noah. 'Oliver's gone mad!
he'll murder me! he's turned wicious!'

Mr Sowerberry punished Oliver with a thorough drubbing and then ordered him up stairs to his dismal bed. Left alone in the gloomy workshop of the undertaker, Oliver wept and wept, and resolved to run away.

With the first ray of light, he tied up a few scraps of food in a handkerchief, unbarred the door and set out for London.

*London! — that great large place! — nobody —
not even Mr Bumble — could ever find him there.*

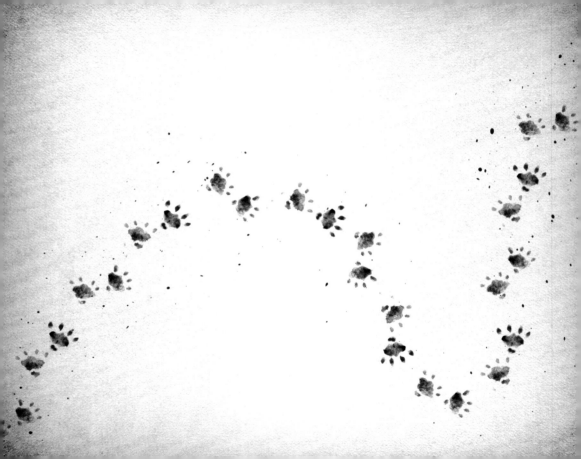

[TO LONDON]

On the way Oliver met the strangest-looking boy that he had ever seen. 'Hullo, my covey,' said this strange young gentleman, 'what's the row?'

'I am very hungry and tired,' Oliver replied. 'I have walked a long way, – I have been walking these seven days.'

'Sivin days! come, you want grub, and you shall have it.'

Among his intimate friends he was better known by the sobriquet of 'The Artful Dodger'.

The Artful Dodger led Oliver to a gloomy room in the dirtiest part of London, where Oliver encountered a very old man by the name of Fagin, whose villainous-looking face was obscured by a quantity of matted hair.

Dressed in a greasy tattered coat, Fagin was dividing his attention between a frying pan of sausages and a clothes-line, over which a great number of silk handkerchiefs were hanging.

'We are very glad to see you, Oliver — very,' said Fagin.

Fagin craftily inducted young Oliver into the pick-pocketing trade, and one morning sent him out to work with the Dodger. The boys walked along to Clerkenwell Green, where they saw an old gentleman reading at a book stall.

'*A prime plant,*' observed the Dodger.

The Dodger plunged his hand into the old gentleman's pocket, withdrew a handkerchief, and then ran away at full speed.

Horrified, Oliver took to his heels as the gentleman turned sharp around. Seeing Oliver scudding away at such a rapid pace, the gentleman shouted—

'STOP THIEF!'

After a helter-skelter chase, Oliver was caught and sentenced to three months' hard labour, until the old gentleman – whose name was Mr Brownlow – persuaded the magistrate that Oliver was innocent.

Exhausted, Oliver fell heavily to the floor in a fainting fit: his face was deadly white, and a cold tremble convulsed his whole frame. Taking pity on the boy, Mr Brownlow took him home to Pentonville.

Weak and thin and pallid, Oliver awoke at last and looked anxiously around.

Mr Brownlow tended Oliver with kindness and solicitude until his fever was quite passed, and then, requiring some books to be returned, sent the young boy out on an errand.

Dressed in a new suit and with a five-pound note buttoned into his jacket pocket, Oliver left the house with the bundle of books.

Accidentally turning down a street which was not in his way, he was claimed by Nancy and Bill Sikes, associates of Fagin.

*Darkness had set in; it was a low neighbourhood;
no help was near; resistance was useless.*

Fagin kept Oliver locked up and alone for many days, until one morning the Dodger asked Oliver to apply himself to 'japanning his trotter-cases' (in plain English: cleaning his boots).

As Oliver worked, the Dodger tried to persuade him to take up the trade again.

'Why don't you put yourself under Fagin, Oliver?' the Dodger said. 'If you don't take handkerchiefs, some other cove will.'

'You've been brought up bad,' said the Dodger, surveying his boots with much satisfaction. 'Fagin will make something of you, though.'

The Dodger was right: Fagin had a plan for Oliver. He gave the boy to Bill Sikes, who was in the house-breaking business and required a boy just Oliver's size for a crack in the far-off village of Chertsey.

When they reached the house, Oliver was shoved through a small lattice window and instructed to unbolt the street-door. But then there was a flash – a loud noise – a smoke – and he staggered back.

'Damnation!' cried Sikes. 'They've hit him!'

Realising that the game was up, Sikes abandoned the wounded boy and made good his escape.

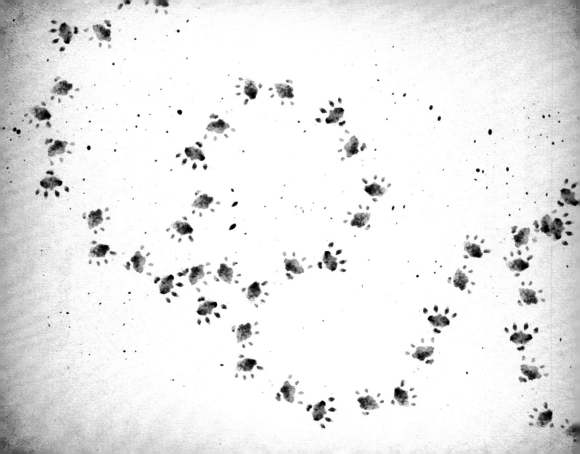

[TO THE COUNTRYSIDE]

Fortunately, Oliver was rescued by the kindly Mr Brownlow and taken to the countryside, where he grew stout and healthy, and learned to read better and to write.

Morning after morning Oliver scoured the country for flowers,
and brought home the fairest that blossomed.

One day Oliver went into a nearby village to deliver a letter. Crossing the inn yard, he accidentally stumbled into a tall man wrapped up in a cloak, whose name was Monks.

Monks advanced towards Oliver, glaring at the boy with his large dark eyes. Even though to Oliver he was a total stranger, he seemed to know the boy…

'Curses on your head, and black death on your heart, you imp! what are you doing here?'

The encounter did not dwell in Oliver's recollection for long, however, for he was labouring hard at his education. One beautiful evening, Oliver sat at his desk and began poring over his books; but the day being uncommonly sultry, he gradually fell asleep.

As he slept, Oliver knew perfectly well that he was in his own little room, but suddenly the scene changed, and he thought with a glow of terror that he was back in Fagin's lair. He awoke and – good God!

There — at the window — there stood Fagin — and beside him, Monks!

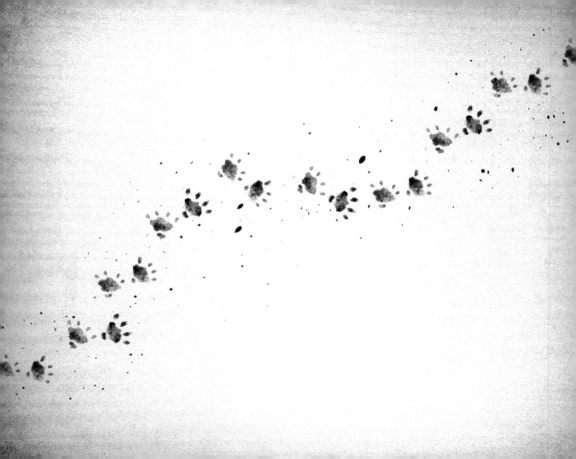

[TO LONDON, AGAIN]

B ack in the city, meanwhile, Nancy had a sudden change of heart. Wanting to help Oliver, she met Mr Brownlow in secret upon London Bridge and told him all about the plan Fagin and Monks had hatched.

'Monks struck a bargain with Fagin,' Nancy said, 'that Fagin was to have money for making Oliver a criminal. Monks wanted the boy hanged for a capital felony; for he said that he was Oliver's brother, and he wanted their father's inheritance all for himself.'

'His brother!' exclaimed Mr Brownlow, clasping his hands.

'Those were his words,' said Nancy, 'but it is growing late, and I must go back, because among all the desperate men I have told you of, there is one that I can't leave – Bill Sikes.'

But Fagin found out that Nancy had blabbed, and made Sikes so angry that he murdered poor Nancy.

Of all the bad deeds that had been committed, that was the worst;
— of all the horrors, that was the most cruel.

Fortunately, however, Mr Brownlow apprehended Monks and made him confess his plot against Oliver.

'I swore,' said Monks, 'that I would hunt him down and bring him, if I could, to the very gallows-foot.'

'Oliver came in my way at last; I began well, and but for a babbling drab
I would have finished as I began; I would, I would!'

Fagin and Sikes both hanged for their crimes.

GUILTY.

What little remains can be told in few and simple words. Oliver came into his rightful inheritance and Mr Brownlow adopted the young boy as his own son, watching with pride as Oliver showed the thriving seeds of all he could wish him to become.

Oliver's warm and earnest heart was perfectly happy at last.

CHARLES DICKENS was born in 1812 and became the most popular novelist of the Victorian era. A prolific writer, he published more than a dozen novels in his lifetime, including *Oliver Twist*, *Great Expectations* and *Hard Times*, most of which have been adapted many times over for radio, stage and screen.

TESS NEWALL was born in 1987 and when she is not sewing miniature tweed caps or paving tiny cobbled streets, she works as a freelance set designer on a variety of scales for fashion, film, events and window displays. She lives in London.

ALEX GOODWIN was born in 1985 and has an MA in Creative Writing from the University of East Anglia, where he surprised his classmates with the news that his first book would feature guinea pigs in bonnets and top hats. He lives in London.

The publishers would like to thank Pauline, Amanda and
Sophia, as well as Charles, Caroline, Jane, Barbara and
the National Forest Adventure Farm for their continuing
comradeship and endless good cheer. Thanks also to the kindly
carpenter, Alfred, for lending his skills to this project. A special
thank you is due, as ever, to the mysterious Belmondo.

Small pets are abandoned every day, but the lucky ones end up
in rescue centres where they can be looked after and rehomed.
You may not know it, but some of these centres are devoted
entirely to guinea pigs. They work with welfare organizations to
give first class advice and information, as well as finding loving
new owners for the animals they look after. If little Oliver Twist
has melted your heart over the course of his adventures, perhaps
think of supporting your local rescue centre!

Bloomsbury Publishing
An imprint of Bloomsbury Publishing Plc

50 Bedford Square
London
WC1B 3DP
UK

1385 Broadway
New York
NY 10018
USA

www.bloomsbury.com

British Library Cataloguing-in-Publication Data
A catalogue record for this book is available from the British Library.

Library of Congress Cataloguing-in-Publication data has been applied for.

ISBN UK:
HB: 978-1-4088-8126-2
EPUB: 978-1-4088-8125-5

ISBN US:
HB: 978-1-63286-708-7
EPUB: 978-1-63286-709-4

2 4 6 8 10 9 7 5 3

Costume, props & illustration: Tess Newall   Photography & book design: Belmondo

Printed and bound in China by C&C Offset Printing Co., Ltd

All papers used by Bloomsbury Publishing are natural, recyclable materials made from wood grown in well-managed forests. The manufacturing processes conform to the environmental regulations of the country of origin.